PEACE

Titles in Papercuts:

QUEEN OF FLIES
TIM COLLINS

SCISSOR MAN
TIM COLLINS

SIGNAL
TIM COLLINS

WAXWORK
TIM COLLINS

PEACE
STEPH CROWLEY

THAW
STEPH CROWLEY

A LITTLE SECRET
ANN EVANS

VIRAL
ANN EVANS

DARK TIDE
JON MAYHEW

THE LANE
IAIN MCLAUGHLIN

BIOLOGY
EMMA NORRY

WILD
EMMA NORRY

MIRRORS
KATE ORMAND

ONE WAY
KATE ORMAND

THE TRICK
KATE ORMAND

ALICE
DANNY PEARSON

THE SICKNESS
JACQUELINE RAYNER

WANTED
JENNI SPANGLER

Badger Publishing Limited, Oldmedow Road, Hardwick Industrial Estate, King's Lynn PE30 4JJ

Telephone: 01438 791037

www.badgerlearning.co.uk

PEACE

STEPH CROWLEY | JAMES LAWRENCE

'The creatures looked right at the humans
with their black, lifeless eyes.'

Peace ISBN 978-1-78837-525-2

Publisher / Senior Editor: Danny Pearson
Editor: Claire Wood
Copyeditor: Cheryl Lanyon
Designer: Bigtop Design Ltd
Illustration: James Lawrence

2 4 6 8 10 9 7 5 3 1

CHAPTER 1
FLASH

People were the worst.

It was 8.30pm and Emily was cleaning up the fitting rooms at her weekend job. Clothes lay crumpled in corners, tags and broken hangers had been thrown around. Someone had left a half-eaten sandwich on the floor in one cubicle. Tomato sauce dripped onto the carpet and a picture had been drawn on one of the mirrors in marker pen. Guess who'd be cleaning that up?

She straightened out a dress and put it properly on the hanger. She wasn't sure where this one went. Most weekends she worked in footwear, where, again, people were the worst. If she had to see one more person shove their sweaty, sockless feet into —

FLASH!

This wasn't the shop.

The clothes rails and the curtains were gone.

She was in a dimly-lit corridor. The ceiling was low enough to touch. The walls were a plain cream colour, about two metres apart. She was still holding the purple dress on its hanger.

It had to be a dream, although everything seemed so real. The cool fabric of the purple dress, the solid floor. She pinched herself. Wasn't that how you were supposed to tell? But it felt like a pinch, and nothing else happened.

She began to walk because what else could she do? And as she followed the gently curving, blank corridor, she noticed the scent of baking bread.

"Hello?" she called out. But she was alone.

The corridor twisted then became wider. On both sides, tanks were built into the walls like in an aquarium, but not as beautiful. The first was full of large, silver-grey fish, swimming in circles. The next was murky green and seemed to contain only plants and algae. The third contained something which looked unfinished, like a baby in the womb, but it was far too big to be human. She stepped closer to the glass to peer inside.

"It's a baby whale." The voice came from behind her. "Or it will be, eventually. They're studying it."

She spun round to see a boy about her age in baggy shorts and a faded blue T-shirt. A toothbrush poked out of one of the pockets on his shorts.

"I'm Jiro," he said. "You're safe. Come on, I'll show you where the others are."

He began walking and she followed him. He was wearing slippers which slapped on the hard floor with every step.

"Where are we?" asked Emily.

"It's hard to explain," he said. "It's easier to show you."

Faint music drifted from somewhere far away. Something classical, with lots of violins. They followed the corridor until it split and Jiro went left. The walls were different here — flat, not curving — and were hung with paintings. Most of them she recognised. There was a copy of the Mona Lisa, Van Gogh's Sunflowers, and that one of a man with an apple for a face. Along with the great works of art there was a random mixture of photos of cats in fancy dress and pop stars.

"What?" said Emily, tilting her head.

"It's supposed to make us feel at home," said Jiro with a shrug. "They're trying their best."

"Who are?" asked Emily.

The classical music came to an end and, in its place, the Dr Who theme tune started.

"Where are you from?" asked Jiro.

"Scotland," said Emily. "You?"

"Japan," said Jiro.

"Your English is perfect."

"Oh, no, it's the ship translating for you. I'm speaking Japanese."

"Ship?" said Emily.

"Clever, isn't it?" Jiro smiled.

"I'm so confused."

"Through here." They reached a door with no handles. Jiro ran one finger down a long, thin groove in the wall and the door slid open.

Emily stepped through into a meeting room. A large, oval table stood in the centre with chairs around it. Three other teenagers were already inside. A girl with braids and folded arms watched her suspiciously. A boy in an American football jersey had his head down on the table, possibly asleep. Another girl, this one wearing a long dress and a green headscarf, paced along the back of the room. There was another tank here, too, but the glass sides didn't reach the ceiling, and it seemed to be empty.

"Welcome, Emily," said a woman's voice very close to her ear.

Emily turned and found herself nose-to-nose with a woman — sort of. At first glance the smiling woman seemed human, but there was something unreal about her smile. It wasn't a person. A robot, maybe. An android? Emily took a step back.

"You have been chosen as an Earth Ambassador," said the not-woman.

"Right," said Emily.

This had to be a dream of some sort, right?
It couldn't be a joke, it was way too detailed
and complicated. Sometimes people had crazy,
realistic dreams when they had the flu, but Emily
felt fine. Maybe she had bumped her head.
Maybe someone would find her conked out in
the fitting rooms at the shop and they'd all laugh
about it next weekend.

"Everyone take a seat," said the robot.

"I'm fine, actually," said the girl in the headscarf.

The robot's head twisted sharply towards her.
"Humans will sit."

There was something very creepy about the
robot. The face was so close to being right, but
there was something about the way it moved and
spoke which was unsettling. They all sat at the
table without further protest. Emily sat between
Jiro and the girl with braids.

"You may now complete your formal act of greeting," said the robot.

The humans stared at each other.

"I think she means introduce ourselves," said Jiro. "Hello, I'm Jiro."

"Hi, I'm Emily." She realised she was still holding the purple dress, and put it down on the table.

"Anika," said the girl with braids.

"Habiba," said the girl with the headscarf. She nudged the other boy with her elbow and he sat up.

"What?" He seemed annoyed.

"Introduce yourself."

"I'm Bryce."

"Welcome, humans." The robot bowed. "I am the ship's official interface. You may call me Egg."

"Egg? Why?" asked Anika.

"Eggs are familiar to all humans. Our research has shown eggs to be non-threatening." The robot smiled, if you could call it that. "Calling me Egg will make you feel at ease."

"Whatever," said Bryce. "You can't keep us here. Let us go."

"You misunderstand," said Egg. "You are not prisoners. You are guests. We are here to help the planet Earth."

It was weird to dream about something like this. Emily didn't watch sci-fi movies or anything. Spaceships and robots weren't things she ever really thought about. And this was a spaceship… right?

"This is messed up," Bryce continued. "You can't snatch us from our homes and call us guests. We're kids. You'll be arrested."

"By who?" asked Habiba. "The space police?"

Bryce stood up, leaning over the table. "I'm an American citizen, I have rights!"

"Silence!" shouted Egg, though her face didn't change. "The humans will cooperate or the humans will be punished."

Bryce sank back down. Nobody wanted to find out what she meant.

"Your planet is suffering," said Egg. "Pollution levels are dangerous to all life forms. There are wars and acts of cruelty. We have come to solve your problems. We will restore peace to the planet Earth."

If they were going to restore peace, why didn't they just do it? Why take a bunch of kids into a spaceship? Why pick Emily?

"This is the weirdest dream I've ever had," Emily whispered to Jiro.

He frowned. "It's not a dream."

"We have done much research on your planet. We have provided for you perfectly, with all the things humans need to be satisfied." She waved towards the speakers in the ceiling, which were now playing an advert for diet coke. "We fix planets. When a planet has intelligent life, we must give those creatures a say in the solution."

Emily was suspicious. This seemed too familiar. Like when a teacher tried to be cool by asking the kids to suggest class rules, but then used their own rules anyway.

"You will speak on behalf of humans. This is your purpose," said Egg.

"We're kids," said Emily. "Teenagers. I'm not even old enough to vote."

"We know," said Egg. "Older humans have been examined and rejected."

"What does that mean?" asked Anika.

"Older humans were not flexible thinkers. They were selfish. You will do better."

"Who are you?" asked Habiba.

"I am the ship's official interface. You can call me Egg." She bowed again.

"No," said Habiba. "Like, whose ship is this?"

"You will meet the hosts soon. First, we shall enjoy Earth food."

CHAPTER 2
WATCH

"We have researched the preferred food items for humans." Egg laid the table with four types of bread and a bowl of ketchup.

"No thank you," Anika said when she was passed a plate.

"The humans will eat. The humans must eat."

As they picked at the food, a screen came down from the ceiling. They were shown thirty minutes of people decorating cakes and falling off skateboards. Emily was desperate to grab Jiro, or one of the others, and ask them to explain what was going on. But every time she turned away from the screen or tried to whisper, Egg gave her a hard stare. She reminded Emily of Mrs Evans, the history teacher, who would make them work in silence, then glare at them, waiting for the chance to put someone in detention.

Except, Emily had the feeling Egg would do something worse than put them in detention. She tried her best to smile and look interested as a man in the video made roses from yellow icing.

"Please excuse me," said Egg.

The moment Egg stepped out of the room, they all started talking.

"Why are we watching this?" Emily asked, keeping her voice low in case Egg returned.

"They think this is what humans like. They're trying to make us happy," Jiro whispered back.

"Are we in danger?" asked Habiba.

"I don't think so…" said Anika. "If they were going to hurt us, why try to make us happy?"

"How did you all get here?" asked Emily.

"I was asleep," said Anika. "I woke up here."

"I was brushing my teeth," said Jiro, "and then suddenly I wasn't."

"Are they… do you think they're really aliens?" asked Bryce.

"She's definitely not human," said Anika.

Everyone nodded in agreement.

"They must be aliens," said Jiro. "Who else would take five kids from all over the world and pretend to be on an alien spaceship?"

"It could be a prank show," said Bryce.

"What prank show has the technology to zap us out of our beds?" said Habiba.

"They're trying to be nice to us," said Jiro, "so I vote we play along and be nice back."

"I vote we escape," said Bryce.

"Cool," said Emily. "Grab your space rocket and fly us all home then."

Bryce scowled. "They kidnapped us. We should be fighting back."

"They said they wanted to end war and pollution," said Habiba. "We should hear them out."

"What if they're lying?" said Bryce.

"What if they're not?" said Anika. "They've got technology we couldn't dream of on Earth. They teleported us here, and translated all our different languages. They also flew through space to find us in the first place! What if they can help the Earth? Don't we owe it to everyone down there to try?"

"And what if they're planning to chop us up and stick us in tanks and study us?" said Bryce.

They all fell silent. On the screen, a skateboarder hit a railing and rolled on the floor. Canned laughter came from the speakers.

"I agree with Anika," said Emily. "Let's hear what they have to say. We have no idea how to get out of this place anyway, so it's our safest choice."

"Right!" said Jiro.

"Agreed," said Habiba.

"You're all sheep," said Bryce, "and you're going to get us cut up into bits."

There was a humming noise and the door opened. Everyone quickly turned their attention back to the screen. A woman laughed as the host told her she had to ice a wedding cake in under three minutes.

Egg looked at each of them in turn. Emily fixed on a smile and tried to look relaxed.

"The humans are pleased with our entertainment," said Egg, as the video finished and the screen rolled back up into the ceiling.

"Thank you," mumbled Jiro.

"Thanks," said Emily.

"Now the humans are ready to work."

Bryce rose to his feet.

No, no, no, no… sit down, thought Emily.

"We're not doing any work for you. Take us back. Now." Bryce put his hands on his hips.

"We are here to help the Earth," said Egg.

"We don't want your help," said Bryce.

"Shut up," Habiba spoke through gritted teeth. She tugged on Bryce's shirt to make him sit down, but he shook her off.

"Take us back," Bryce repeated.

For several seconds nobody moved. Everyone watched Egg uneasily, waiting to see how she would respond to him.

"Humans resist. Humans are not grateful for our help." She paused. "We have prepared for this."

What did that mean? Was she going to hurt them?

The lights went out. The screen rolled back down from the ceiling. Bryce looked around awkwardly, then sat down.

"Observe," said Egg.

This video was very different from the last. They were not meant to enjoy this one. The first clip was of a polar bear lying flat out on some ice. The bear was thin. Too thin. It was obviously dying. The next clip showed small children picking at an enormous rubbish dump. The third was a lake with water black and thick from pollution and the shore scattered with fish bones. When the screen showed images of injured people in a war zone, Emily looked away.

"The humans will watch," demanded Egg.

The video didn't last long. Ten minutes, maybe less. But by the end all the teenagers were quiet. Emily's eyes stung with tears.

"Do the humans need more proof?" asked Egg.

"No," said Anika. "No more, please."

"We have found an unacceptable level of suffering on Earth. As the dominant species, you must help us fix it. Or do you wish this to continue?"

"No," said Emily. "We'll help."

"Then I shall invite in the hosts," said Egg.

CHAPTER 3
GUESTS

The lights slowly came up.

Egg gave off a sound — a long, high-pitched tone like a broken fire alarm. Emily covered her ears but the sound cut into her brain anyway. It was followed by a series of bleeps, fast and sharp. It could have been Morse code, or it could have been the robot going into self-destruct mode.

When Egg finally stopped, there was a faint clicking and scraping sound, which grew gradually louder. This new sound was coming from the tank of water at the side of the room.

Emily leaned forwards to get a better look. For the first time she noticed there was a hole where the tank met the wall, and the water continued into another room of the ship. Something was coming through it.

Two sticks… No! They were something else. The first stick unfolded and stretched out into a long, thin, three-jointed leg. The second leg unfolded in the same way, and then a third. Then a rounded, shell-covered body came through the hole.

They all gasped as the creature came completely into view. It was like a crab, or a giant spider. Its body was as high as Emily's head, though she suspected it would be much taller if it straightened its legs. The orange-brown body was the size of a beach ball, but flatter and more oval. At the front were two smaller legs, each ending with a huge, long claw.

A second creature came through the gap behind the first. This one was slightly smaller, and more of a blueish colour. Its claws were even bigger.

Egg turned to face the tank and made a strange swaying movement. Emily guessed it was some sort of bow or salute to the creatures. Then Egg spoke to the humans.

"You are honoured to meet our leaders. Most are not so lucky. You will not speak to them directly. They are simply here to observe."

The teenagers nodded. What would they even say to a giant spider-crab alien anyway?

Bryce folded his arms. The video of suffering might have shut him up for the moment, but Emily could tell he hadn't changed his mind about helping. She hoped he wouldn't make things worse.

"Excuse me," said Habiba. "We're very, um, honoured. And grateful. And we want to help the Earth. But I don't understand what we can do. We don't have any power. We're kids. We can't fix any of this."

"We know," said Egg. "We will act on your behalf. But we need your ideas. Our world is not your world. Our culture is not your culture. We cannot make things right on Earth if we do not know how Earth decides what is right and what is wrong."

"I get it," said Jiro. "If they don't understand what we think, they might do something really awful because they're trying to help."

"This human is correct," said Egg.

"So we just need to explain what's right and what's wrong?" asked Emily. That didn't sound so bad. "And then you'll let us go?"

"The humans are not prisoners," said Egg. "The humans are honoured guests."

Bryce opened his mouth and Habiba elbowed him in the side before he could argue.

"OK," said Anika. "What do you need to know?"

"Let's begin with something easy. How do you teach your young not to do bad things?" Egg asked with a smile. Behind her the bodies of the aliens gently bobbed up and down in the water. Were they listening? Did they understand?

"You tell them to stop," said Habiba.

"And your young always obey?" asked Egg.

"All kids are naughty sometimes," said Habiba.

"Then how do you deal with this bad behaviour?"

"Punish them," said Jiro. "Send them to bed early."

"Or take away something they like," added Emily. "Like sweets or toys."

"I understand," said Egg. "We have similar methods. And how do you decide which actions should be punished?"

"We just sort of… know," said Anika.

"Give examples," said Egg.

"Stealing," said Jiro. "If you take something which doesn't belong to you. Without permission."

"Stealing is wrong," repeated Egg.

"Not always," said Habiba. "If you had to steal food because your family was starving, it wouldn't be wrong."

"Yes it would," said Anika.

"You're saying you would let them starve?" Habiba turned her chair towards Anika.

"No. I'm saying it's still wrong, even though you're doing it for a good reason."

"Right," said Jiro. "Sometimes all the choices are wrong, so you have to do the thing that's least wrong."

"This is stupid," said Bryce. "I thought aliens were supposed to be super smart? Why do we need to explain stealing to a bunch of crabs?"

"Shh!" said Habiba.

"Is it wrong to ignore someone who needs help?" asked Egg.

"Yes," said Emily.

"No," said Jiro. "Not always. Not if you can't help them, or if someone else would be hurt because you helped."

"Fine," said Emily. "But almost always, you should help if you can. That's what being a good person means. You should do everything you can to make people suffer less."

"Great," said Bryce. "Lesson over. Now send us home."

"Our work is not over," said Egg.

"No, you're finished. You want to know about right and wrong? Taking people into space without asking is wrong." Bryce was on his feet again.

The aliens seemed interested — as much as Emily could guess their feelings — pressing closer to the glass of their tank and making clicking noises with their claws.

"I understand," said Egg, then went silent.

Something changed in the air. No, the air itself changed. There had been a gentle flow of air through the vents in the ceiling, and it had stopped. The soft hum of fans had stopped too.

"What happened?" asked Habiba.

"We have taken action according to your moral code."

"What does that mean?" asked Emily. It was something bad. She knew it was something bad.

"It is wrong to refuse to help those who suffer. Wrong behaviour must be punished. This human refuses to help the Earth. As punishment we have taken away something he likes."

"What? What have you taken away?" yelled Bryce. His eyes were wide with panic.

"Oxygen," said Egg. "Our studies show that oxygen is the thing humans most like."

"Need," said Emily. "Oxygen is what we need. You can't take it away. We'll die!"

There was a ripple of panic throughout the room. Bryce ran over to the door and tried to open it, but it wouldn't budge. He began pulling at it, but his fingers couldn't grip the smooth surface.

"Stay calm," said Jiro. "The more we panic, the quicker the oxygen will run out."

"It's OK," said Anika. "We're OK. In a room this big, it'll take us days to use up all the oxygen."

"You are correct," said Egg. "So I will remove it all, to teach the humans a lesson."

The fans in the air vents whirred back to life, but this time they were sucking air out of the room.

Emily tried to breathe slowly and calmly, but it felt strange, like the air was thick, like she was breathing underwater. Pressure built inside her chest and throat. She gasped and spluttered, trying to pull in as much air as she could, but her heart was beating faster and faster. Jiro was clutching his chest. Habiba put her head in her hands. Over by the door, Bryce sank down to his knees.

"Please stop," said Anika. "Please!"

"I'm sorry," said Bryce between gasps. "I'm sorry."

CHAPTER 4
SACRIFICE

"Very good," said Egg. "We shall allow you to have oxygen."

The direction of the fans changed and within moments the crushing feeling in Emily's chest started to ease.

"Return to your seats," said Egg, and everyone did as they were told. They sat in a stunned and terrified silence.

In the tank, the two creatures clicked their mouth parts together and made a chattering noise. It was almost like they were laughing.

Emily's hands were shaking. She wasn't cold, but she was trembling all over. She held on tightly to the arms of her chair, trying to steady herself. Bryce was staring down at his feet. Anika reached over and held Habiba's hand.

"Stealing is bad," said Egg. "Please explain what other actions are unacceptable on Earth."

"Um…" Jiro rubbed his head. "Killing."

"Humans kill for food," said Egg.

"What?" said Emily.

"We kill for food," said Anika.

"Not everyone," said Habiba.

"But it's different when it's for food," said Emily. "Lots of animals eat other animals."

"Some animals don't have a choice," said Habiba. "Humans do."

"We evolved to eat animals," said Bryce, piping up for the first time since the oxygen was switched back on. "You can't blame us for that."

"But we evolved to be smart. We can find what we need without killing," said Habiba.

"You wouldn't blame a lion for eating a gazelle," said Bryce.

The aliens were bobbing faster, clicking their claws together. They seemed to be excited when the humans were upset.

"Lions are carnivores," Anika said. "We're omnivores."

"Exactly — OMNI-vores, which means we eat everything — plants and meat." Bryce was getting louder.

"Silence," said Egg. "Killing for food is acceptable, yes or no?"

"No," said Habiba.

"Yes," said Bryce.

"Sometimes," said Jiro.

"Sometimes it is acceptable to kill," said Egg.

"Only if it prevents more death," said Emily. She didn't want to give Egg any ideas — if they weren't careful, she'd decide it was OK to cut off the oxygen forever and suffocate them all. "You would kill a lion if it was going to eat a bunch of children."

"Or if you could go back in time and kill some future tyrant or dictator as a baby," said Bryce.

"It is acceptable to kill infants?" asked Egg.

"No!" said Anika.

"If you knew it would be a tyrant or dictator, when it grew up, that's different," said Bryce.

"The Earth has terrible wars," said Egg. "Many people die. To us, this seems wrong. Do humans want war to continue?"

"Of course not," said Habiba.

"War is always wrong," said Jiro.

"Is it?" said Emily. "I mean, if some dictator does terrible things, shouldn't someone stop them? If you ignore them, they could kill thousands of people. Maybe a war is better than letting that happen."

"Killing during war is acceptable?" asked Egg.

"It's more complicated than that," said Jiro. "We can't just tell you yes and no. Maybe this is simple where you come from. It's not simple for us. Sometimes things can be right in one situation and wrong in another."

"Sometimes all the answers are bad," said Habiba.

"Explain," said Egg.

"We are trying to explain!" snapped Bryce.

The smaller alien tapped on the glass with a claw, pointing towards Bryce. Egg turned her face towards him and he shrank back into his chair like a frightened puppy.

"Why can you not give us a simple answer?" said Egg. "We are trying to help you. Do you need to be reminded of the suffering?"

The screen began descending from the ceiling.

"No!" said Emily. "Please. We're trying. It's hard to explain. It's like…" she thought back to something she had seen on a TV show once, "… the trolley problem!"

She looked around to the others for support but they all stared at her blankly. She swallowed hard, her mouth dry.

"Imagine you're driving a trolley-bus or a train and the brakes have failed. It's going to hit five workmen on the track ahead. They will all die. Or, you can flip a switch to move the train onto another track where it will only kill one person. Should you do it?"

"Yes," said Anika. "Obviously."

"Save five lives, sacrifice one," said Bryce.

"And then there's more parts to the problem. Like, what if the one person was someone you loved?"

"You should still do it," Habiba said.

"But would you, though? Could you?" said Jiro. "It's easy to say you'd do it, but could you actually do it?"

"Or, what if it was one pregnant woman or five old people? Or one…" she grasped for examples, "… one endangered polar bear versus five pet dogs."

"Why would a polar bear be on the train tracks?" said Bryce.

"Whatever," said Emily. "The next question is, what if you're a doctor and you have five patients who will each die without a different organ transplant? And then you have one healthy person who is a match for all five and could give all of them the organs they need. Should you murder the one healthy person to save the other five?"

"No," said Habiba. "You can't murder someone."

"But switching the train tracks would be murder too, wouldn't it?" Emily sat forwards on the edge of her chair. "The single person was going to be fine, until you decided to kill them."

"But the five workmen were going to be killed," said Bryce.

"And the patients will die if they don't get organs," said Jiro. "I get it. But it feels different, the patients are dying of something natural."

"But you could save all five patients. Wouldn't that be a better result for the world?" said Emily.

"Would you do it?" asked Habiba.

"No," said Emily. "I don't think I could. But that's my point. It's not simple. You could argue both ways."

"What if you could kill a man who would become a serial killer and save five victims?" said Bryce. "Would you do it?"

"Maybe," said Anika. "If I knew for sure he was going to kill five people."

"Even if he was only going to kill one," said Bryce, "it'd be worth it. Because it's better to save an innocent person than a murderer."

"But if he hasn't killed anyone yet, he's not a murderer," said Emily.

"Some lives are worth more than other lives," said Egg. "Yes?"

"No," said Emily. "Maybe."

"Yes," said Anika. "Someone who does a lot of harm to others is less valuable."

Jiro looked uncomfortable. "I suppose so. But people deserve second chances."

Both aliens raised their bodies up over the water line and made a quick series of squeaks and taps. Egg waved back to them as if accepting an order.

"What is the correct answer?" asked Egg.

"To what?" asked Anika.

"To the trolley problem."

"There isn't one," said Emily. "That's the point. It's too complicated."

"We must have an answer," said Egg. "Perhaps this will help you to decide."

The fans once again whirred to a stop.

"No, please!" said Jiro. "Not again."

"I will not remove the oxygen, but you will receive no more until you give us the answer," said Egg. "Based on the size of the room and your needs, you will lose consciousness in twenty-one hours."

CHAPTER 5
REWARD

Egg left the room.

The crab creatures continued to watch from inside their tank. The creatures looked right at the humans with their black, lifeless eyes. Like dolls' eyes. Sometimes they made their strange clicking sound. From time to time they banged on the glass. Habiba turned her chair away from the tank so she couldn't see them. What were they looking for?

Emily's heart was pounding. She tried not to think about the oxygen running out. The best thing to do was stay calm. They only needed to give Egg an answer to the trolley problem.

It wasn't as easy as it sounded. Each time four of them agreed, one person would bring up a new argument. For the most part, they thought the best thing would be to save as many people as possible. But they couldn't quite agree which was the best of all the possible variations.

After they had argued for thirty minutes or so, the larger of the two creatures poked a long, spindly leg over the top of the tank.

"Um… guys," said Emily. "Look."

A second leg came over the edge of the tank and the creature raised itself up, its body coming out of the water like a submarine.

"We're going to be eaten!" said Bryce. "I told you we needed to get out of here."

Each leg set itself down with a hard click until the creature was entirely out of the water. It moved smoothly. Its body stayed perfectly level as the legs went up and down around it.

"Make it stop," said Emily under her breath.

"Egg!" shouted Jiro. "We're ready. We have an answer."

"Egg?" Anika joined in with the shouting. The creature was beside her now. The long claw prodded at her face and she shivered in disgust. It lowered its body to be level with her face and made the clicking noise.

The door opened and Egg entered.

"Egg, what's happening?" asked Emily. "Why is it doing that?"

"You are honoured. He is pleased with your discussions," said Egg.

"We've decided," said Jiro. "The answer to the trolley problem. You should flip the switch, right? If you can't save everyone, save as many lives as possible."

He looked around to the others. They nodded. Yes. They wanted it to stop. The creature was now holding some of Anika's braids in its claw.

"Do you all agree?" asked Egg.

"Yes," said Habiba.

"Yes," said Bryce.

The crab creature dropped Anika's braids and talked to Egg in its quick chatter.

"The hosts thank you for your cooperation. You will be rewarded."

"Please," said Emily, "we want to go home."

"Did we do it?" asked Habiba. "Are you going to save the Earth?"

"Yes," said Egg. "We have the information we need. We will bring peace to Earth."

The crab creature slowly climbed back into its tank. The smaller one folded itself up and went through the hole in the side of the tank and out of sight. The larger one followed.

"You may follow the lit passageway to the viewing deck," said Egg. "You may watch us save the Earth. Oxygen will be provided."

Egg left and the speakers began playing music again. This time it was music from the film The Wizard of Oz — Somewhere Over the Rainbow.

"Shall we go?" asked Jiro.

"Yes, I think we should do as we're told," said Habiba. "We don't want to make them angry again."

They left the room and followed a glowing red line in the ceiling through the twisting tunnels of the ship.

Here and there were more tanks of water and Emily kept watch for the crab-creatures, but she didn't see any.

When they reached a dead end, the panels of the wall slid aside and let them into a room with a whole wall of windows.

It looked out into the blackness of space.

Floating in the centre of their view was the Earth, a blue-green marble surrounded by a paper-thin layer of atmosphere.

"Wow," said Emily. "This is incredible!"

"It looks so fragile when you see it from up here," said Habiba.

Egg stepped forwards from a shadowy corner.

"You are just in time to watch. Thanks to your information, we have decided on the best way to restore peace and balance to the Earth."

"What will you do?" asked Jiro.

"Save as many lives as we can, by sacrificing others."

"Uh, what?" said Anika. "Sacrificing… who?"

"All of them," said Egg.

Cold shock ran down Emily's back. She knew she had to ask, but she was afraid she already knew the answer. "All of who?"

"The humans." Egg smiled.

"But, that's billions of people!" said Bryce.

"You can't!" shouted Jiro.

"It is the right thing to do. Sacrifice their lives to save countless billions of other animals. Humans are the cause of pollution and war. The Earth's atmosphere will recover. The ecosystem will return to balance. The Earth will be saved. Thanks to you."

"No!" begged Emily.

The first beam hit the Earth. Egg laughed.

THE END